Story Time

By Jean Warren

Illustrated by Susan True

Publisher: Roberta Suid
Editor: Bonnie Bernstein
Design: David Hale
Cover art: Corbin Hillam

The author wishes to thank Sue Foster
for her contribution of the rhyme "Five Little Froggies"
and Anita Halstead for her contribution of the "Story Codes" idea.

ISBN 0-912107-16-2

Printed in the United States of America

9 8 7 6 5 4 3 2 1

PREFACE

A fill-in-the-blanks storytelling format leaves wide open the possibilities for language expansion in this collection of original stories, songs, rhymes, and problem-solving scenarios.

Young children need a balance of language experiences. They need structured activities to learn correct usage and pronunciation, but they also need open-ended activities which will help them use language to solve problems and create new ideas. **Story Time** is an attempt to show parents and teachers how several creative framing devices can turn a young child's everyday experiences into exotic language experiences, and also offer structural models. Unlike the blind responses generated in many fill-in word games, the responses children make in **Story Time** frames follow a theme and a progression. Although the lead-in text for the activities in no way limits the content (or often the length) of the children's responses, it is written in such a way as to encourage the children to develop their ideas as they follow along.

The **Story Time** activities can be used with many children in a circle, or one child on a lap, and children can participate differently according to their ages and abilities: preschoolers can listen and respond verbally; and older children can read and respond in writing. The important thing is to encourage and accept as "correct" all responses, even the absurd ones. Especially in the problems section, where they are asked to make choices, contemplate alternatives, and experiment with possible solutions, the children should feel free to contribute without worrying about limitations or consequences. In this unconditional atmosphere, the children will experience immediate success and have the confidence to be creative and open in their answers.

Many of the activities in this book were compiled from ideas featured in the **Totline**, a 24-page bi-monthly newsletter. The **Totline** regularly features preschool activities in the following areas: art, creative movement, coordination, language development, learning games, science, and self-awareness. Each issue also includes holiday party ideas, sugarless snack recipes, and a special infant-toddler ideas section. For more information, write: Warren Publishing House, P.O. Box 2255, Everett, WA 98203.

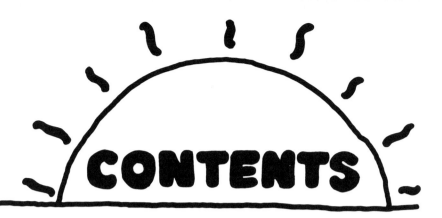

CONTENTS

STORIES

The Zoo

I love the zoo.
There are so many animals
to see.
The silliest animal is the
_____.
The tallest animal is the
_____.
The smallest animal is the
_____.
The most friendly animal is the
_____.
The fattest animal is the _____.
The noisiest animal is the _____.
The cleanest animal is the _____.
The prettiest animal is the _____.
My favorite animal is the _____.
If we had room, I would like to keep
a _____ in my yard.

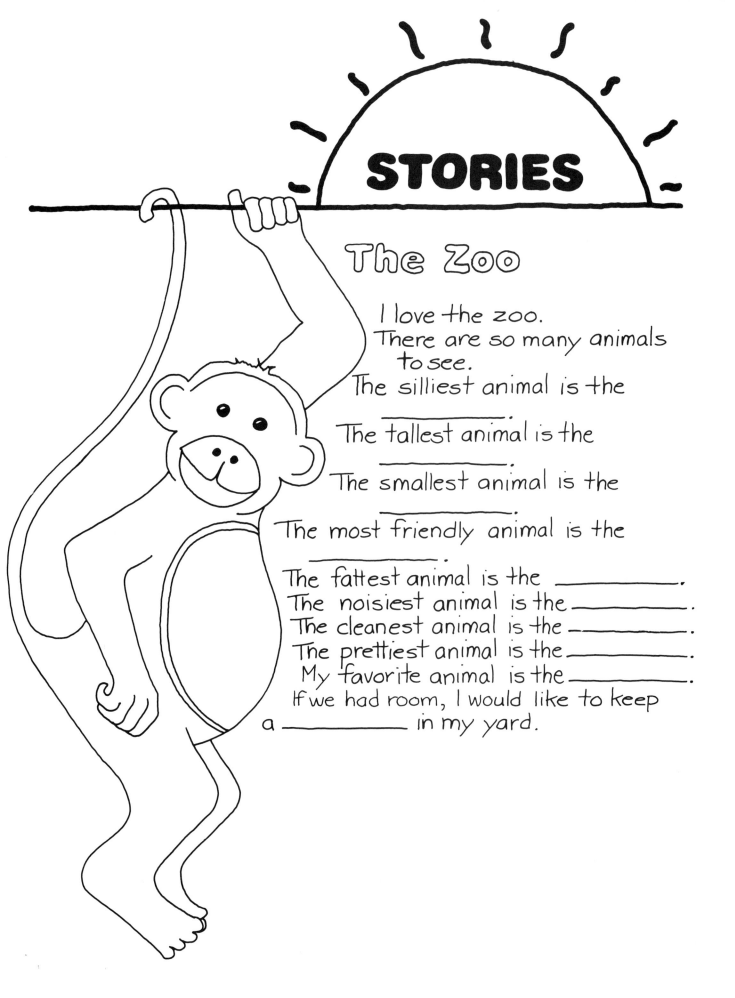

My Sandwich

I'm making myself a sandwich.
First I take out two pieces of _____ .
Next I spread on some _____ .
Then I add a _____ .
Next come two pieces of _____ ,
    then some _____ and a sprinkle
    of _____ .
Mmmm, it looks so good!
I put everything on top of each other and
    then top it off with _____ .
I like to make my own sandwich.

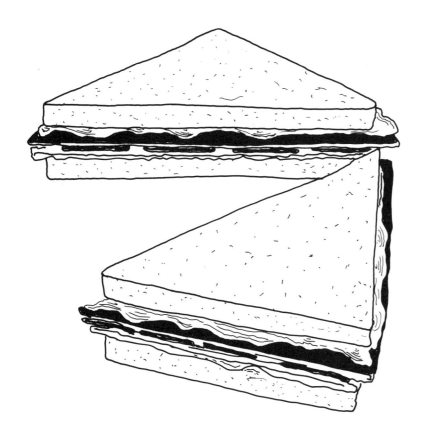

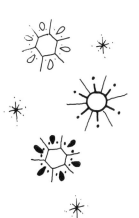

My Snowman

I have fun when it snows.
I can make a snowman as round as a
_____.

I can make a face for my snowman
with _____.
I can make arms for my snowman
with _____.
I know my snowman is happy because
_____.

I am going to name my snowman
_____.

My snowman is my friend.

Clouds

I sat watching the clouds today.
A great big cloud reminded me of a
_____.
Another one made me hungry because it
looked like _____.
Another one was round like a _____.
Next to it was a cloud that looked like a
stuffed _____.
The cloud I liked best looked like
_____.

I like looking at the clouds.

14

The Beach

I went to the beach today.
 The sun was as hot as _____.
 The sky was as blue as _____.
The water was as cold as _____.
I swam in the water just like a _____.
I played in the sand and built a _____.
While I was digging in the sand, I found a
 _____.
I love to run on the beach like a _____.
I had fun at the beach.

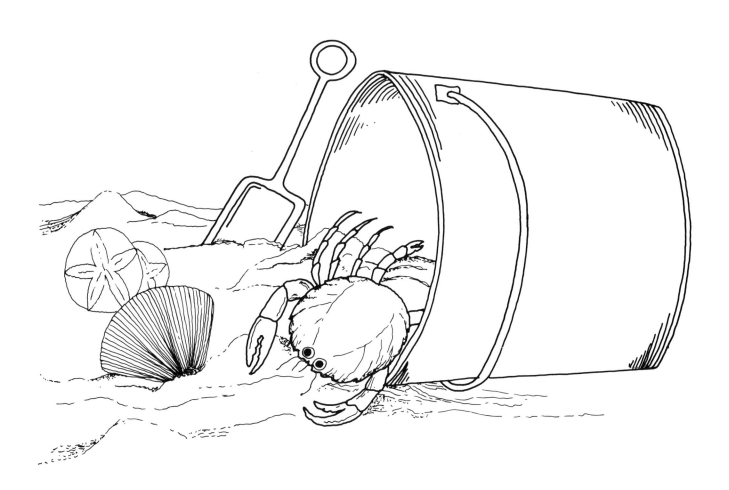

Surprises

Sometimes surprises are round like a
_____.

Sometimes surprises are wrapped up
like a _____.

Sometimes surprises are loud like
_____.

Sometimes surprises are small like
_____.

Sometimes surprises are cold like
_____.

Sometimes surprises are
funny like _____.

I like surprises!

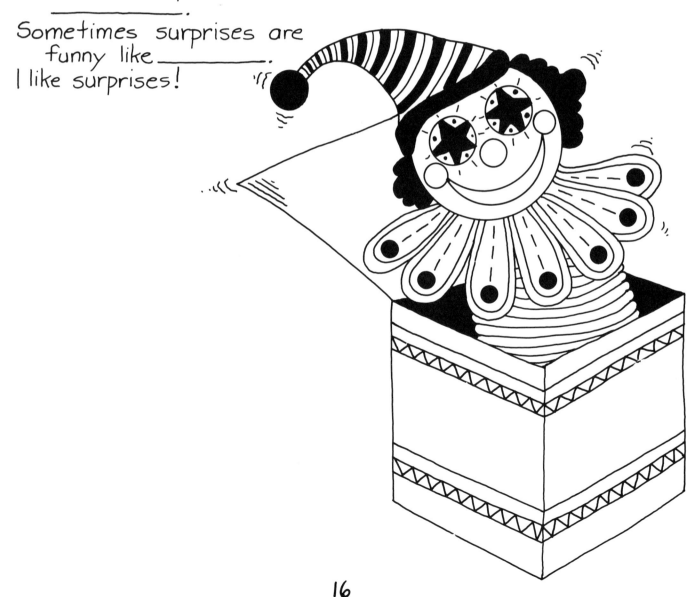

16

Happy Birthday

It is my birthday.
I feel as old as _____.
I am happy because _____.
I think I will wear my _____ today.
My cake looks like a _____.
I hope we have ice cream that tastes
    like _____.
What I really want for my birthday
    is _____.
I opened a small present. It was a
    _____.
I opened a big present. It was a
    _____.
Birthdays make me feel _____.
I wish it was my birthday every day!

17

Toys

I am shopping for a toy.
The biggest toy I see is a _____.
The funniest toy I see is a _____.
Some toys can move; the one I like
    best is _____.
The smallest round toy I see is a _____.
The softest toy I see is a _____.
Some toys you play with outside; the one
    I like best is _____.
Some toys you can take to bed with you;
    the one I like best is the _____.
Some toys you can play with by yourself;
    the one I like best is the _____.
Some toys you need other people to play
    with; the one I like best is the _____.
The toy I would most like to buy is _____.

The Christmas Tree

I love to sit and look at our Christmas tree.
It makes me happy because _____.
My favorite ornament is a _____.
The lights sparkle like _____.
The bulbs are round like _____.
At the top we put a _____.
I like to help put on the _____.
When I see the tree all lit up, it makes me
want to _____.
I love looking at our Christmas tree.

19

Homemade Cookies

I love to help make cookies.
Sometimes the dough smells like _____.
When I roll out the dough it looks like a great
    big _____.
My favorite cookie cutter is the _____.
The biggest cookie I ever made was a
    _____.

The smallest cookie I ever made looked like a
    _____.

After we bake the cookies, I frost them.
I put _____ frosting on some of the
    cookies and _____ frosting on others.
The most beautiful cookie I ever made was a

    _____.

The funniest cookie I ever made was a
    _____.

Making cookies is fun, but eating them is
    even more fun.

Box Rides

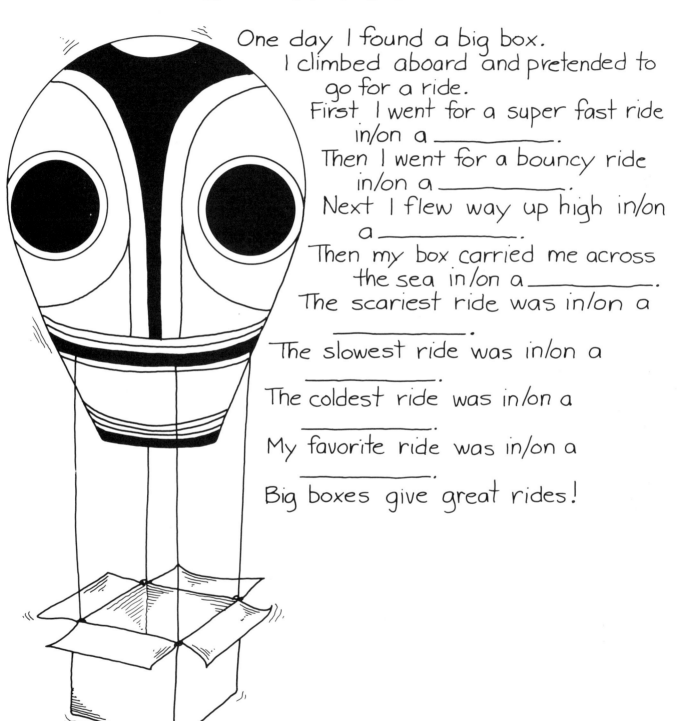

One day I found a big box.
I climbed aboard and pretended to go for a ride.
First I went for a super fast ride in/on a _____.
Then I went for a bouncy ride in/on a _____.
Next I flew way up high in/on a _____.
Then my box carried me across the sea in/on a _____.
The scariest ride was in/on a _____.

The slowest ride was in/on a _____.

The coldest ride was in/on a _____.

My favorite ride was in/on a _____.

Big boxes give great rides!

Symbol Stories

Symbol stories encourage children to use their imaginations. Set up a story line, using symbols such as circles, squares and wavy lines. The child assigns a word to each symbol. Additional words can be used between symbols to connect the story ideas. Start with simple one-line stories, then gradually "write" your children longer symbol stories to decode however they wish.

Example: □ □ ～ ○ ●●● △

One child may "read" the symbol story above something like this:
   "The mother bear and the baby bear ran down to the lake. They caught three fish and took them home."
   Another child may read the symbol story above something like this:
   "The truck and the little car drove over the mountain and stopped at a big town. They stayed three days and then went home."
   What kind of stories can the children tell using the symbols below?

24

SONGS

Smells Like Dinner

(Sung to "Frère Jacques")

Smells like dinner
Smells like dinner
Mmmm, Mmmm good!
Mmmm, Mmmm good!
I can smell the _____
I can smell the _____
Mmmm, Mmmm good!
Mmmm, Mmmm good!

The children fill in their favorite dinner smells. Then repeat the song for breakfast, lunch, and holiday feasts, such as Thanksgiving, Christmas, or Passover.

Today Is Monday

(Sung to "Mary Had A Little Lamb")

Today is (a)_____ day, _____
    day, _____ day
Today is (a) _____ day, let's all sing
    a song.
It will be a fun day, fun day, fun day,
It will be a fun day, all day long.
Let's sing about (a) _____ day, _____
    day, _____ day,
Let's sing about (a) _____, all day long.

Change the word in the blank to fit the day.
Examples:
    Monday, Tuesday, etc.
    Birthday, Holiday, Valentine's Day
    Sunny day, Windy day, etc.
    Blue day, Red day, etc.

26

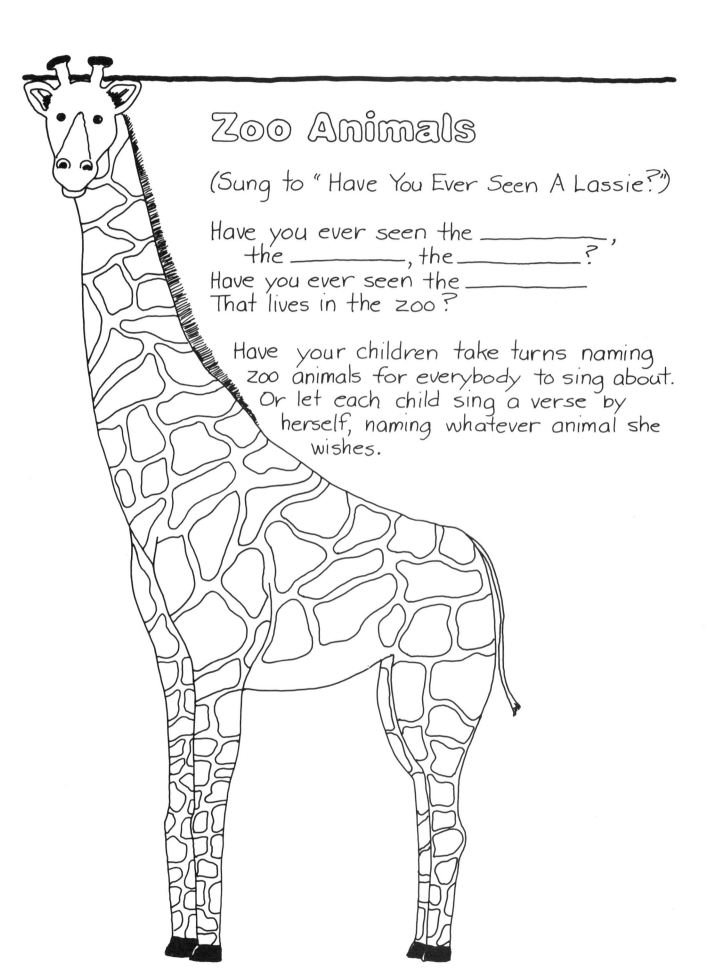

Zoo Animals

(Sung to "Have You Ever Seen A Lassie?")

Have you ever seen the _____,
   the _____, the _____?
Have you ever seen the _____
That lives in the zoo?

Have your children take turns naming zoo animals for everybody to sing about. Or let each child sing a verse by herself, naming whatever animal she wishes.

29

Time Song

(Sung to "London Bridge")

Now it's time to _____ _____,

_____ _____ _____;

_____, _____ _____;

_____

Now it's time to _____ _____

_____

For it's _____ o'clock.

Have your children sing about different
times in their day. Examples:
    eat our lunch; for it's twelve o'clock
    go to bed; for it's eight o'clock
    go to school; for it's nine o'clock
    take my bath; for it's seven o'clock
    feed my dog; for it's four o'clock

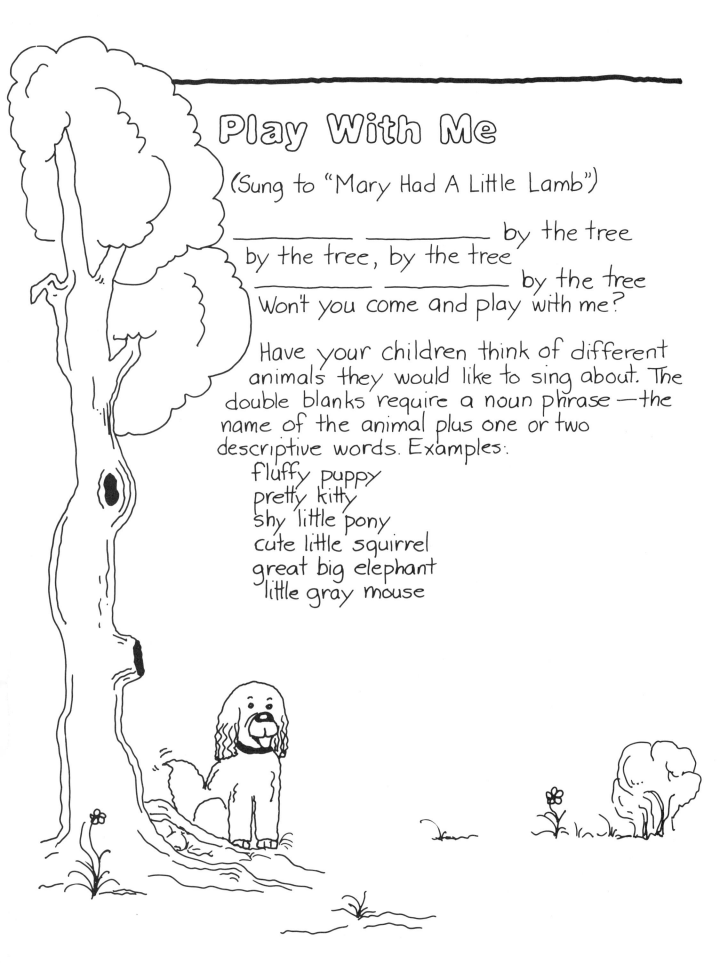

Play With Me

(Sung to "Mary Had A Little Lamb")

_____ _____ by the tree
by the tree, by the tree
_____ _____ by the tree
Won't you come and play with me?

Have your children think of different animals they would like to sing about. The double blanks require a noun phrase—the name of the animal plus one or two descriptive words. Examples:

fluffy puppy
pretty kitty
shy little pony
cute little squirrel
great big elephant
little gray mouse

The Lost Song

(Sung to "Mary Had A Little Lamb")

Do you know where my _____ is?
  my _____ is, my _____ is?
Do you know where my _____ is?
I lost my _____ today.

Have the children take turns thinking of
things to pretend they can't find. Examples:
  pencil   dog
  mitten   mother
  hat   teddy bear
  sweater   teacher

38

The Circle Song

(Sung to "The Wheels On The Bus")

Oh, the _____ on the _____
Go(es) 'round and 'round
'Round and 'round
'Round and 'round
Oh, the _____ on the _____
Go(es) 'round and 'round
All day long.

Have your children fill in things that go around and around. Examples:
  Train on the track
  Fish in the bowl
  Hamster on the wheel
  Ponies in the ring
  Seals in the tank
      Propellers on the plane
      Blades on the fan
      Skaters in the rink
      People on the rides
      Hands on the clock

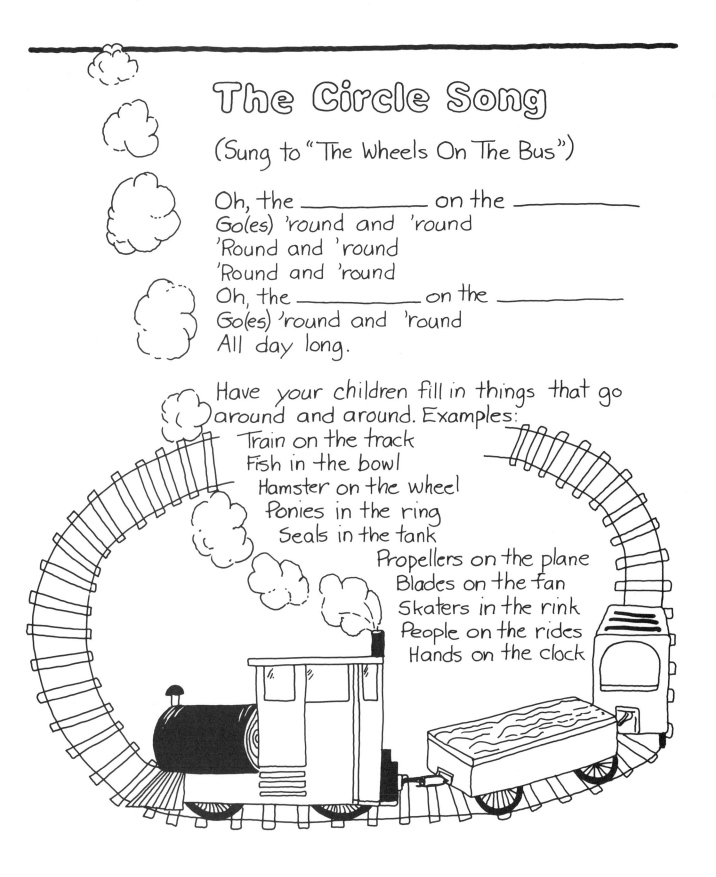

I Hear Dogs Bark

(Sung to "Frère Jacques")

I hear _____
I hear _____
Hear them _____
Hear them _____

_____ _____ _____
_____ _____ _____
_____ _____ _____

Hear them _____.
Hear them _____.

First use this song to sing about band instruments and their sounds, then about animals, and the sounds **they** make. Examples:

Band Instruments
   drums beat
   Rat-a-tat-a-tat-tat
   bells ring
   Ding-a-ling-a-ling-ling
   horns blow
   Toot-a-toot-a-toot-toot

Animals
   dogs bark
   Arf-arf-arf-arf-arf-arf
   cats meow
   Meow-meow-meow-meow-meow-meow
   birds chirp
   Tweet-tweet-tweet-tweet-tweet-tweet

Arf-arf-arf

RHYMES

The Trunk

While searching for treasures the other day.
I found a big trunk packed far away.
I opened the trunk and what did I find?
Wonderful treasures of every kind.
On the top of the pile was a great big

_____.

Then I discovered two old _____.
Next was a shiny black _____.
My favorite was a _____.
The most beautiful treasure was a _____
The bottom of the trunk was filled with

_____.

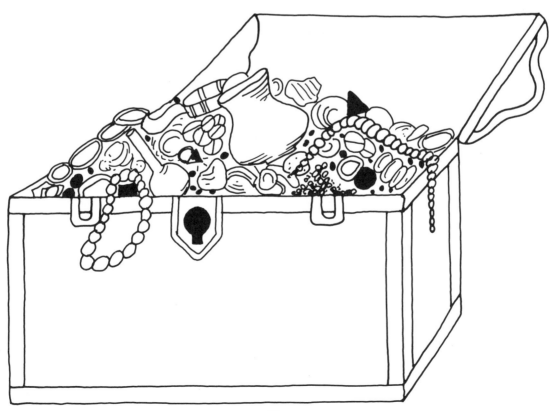

Trick-Or-Treaters

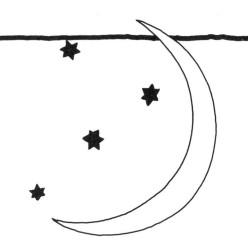

Knock, knock, sounds like more
Trick-or-treaters at my door.
I open the door and what do I see?
Two green _____ smiling at me.

Knock, knock, sounds like more
Trick-or-treaters at my door.
I open the door and what do I see?
A great big _____ smiling at me.

Knock, knock, sounds like more
Trick-or-treaters at my door.
I open the door and what do I see?
A tiny, tiny _____ smiling at me.

Other possible endings:
    An ugly old _____ smiling at me.
    A funny brown _____ smiling at me.
    Three orange _____ smiling at me.
    A big white _____ smiling at me.
    Ten little _____ smiling at me.

44

Vegetable Man

While I was walking down the street,
A vegetable man, I happened to meet.
His head was a bumpy _____.
His arms were long _____.
His body was a large _____.
His legs were two green _____.
His feet were round _____.
His fingers and toes were red _____.
He looked so good that on a hunch
I invited the man home for lunch!

Sunshine

The morning sun peeked through the trees
To kiss the _____ and the honey bees.
It danced by the _____ and the
    fields of hay.
Until it reached the _____
    where it stayed all day.

Sun, sun don't you run
Stay with me and have some fun.
Shine on the _____, shine on me.
Shine on the _____, shine on
    the tree.
Shine on the _____, shine so fair
Shine on the _____, shine everywhere!

46

Old Bombay

Ready, set, go! We're on our way
Off to visit old Bombay.

First we'll ride on a _____ going
    our way
As we travel to old Bombay.

Next we'll catch a _____ going our way
On our journey to old Bombay.

Then we'll hop aboard a _____ going
    our way.
As we travel to old Bombay.

At last we'll jump on a _____ going
    our way
On our journey to old Bombay.

Here we are at last in old Bombay.
Traveling can be fun if you know your way!

Bumble

I have a dog named Bumble
Who lives at home with me.
Sometimes he likes to hide
Then my dog I cannot see.

I looked in the _____.
I looked over the _____.
I looked behind the _____.
I looked under the _____.
Now where can BUMBLE BE?

Waiter, Waiter

Waiter, waiter on the run
I love _____
Bring me one.

Waiter, waiter dressed in blue
I love _____
Bring me two.

Waiter, waiter by the tree
I love _____

Bring me three.

Waiter, waiter by the door
I love _____
Bring me four.

Waiter, waiter, sakes alive
I love _____
Bring me five.

Jumping Jack

Poor, poor Jumping Jack
He jumped so far he never came back.
He jumped over _____.
And he jumped over _____.
He jumped over _____.
And he never came back.

What I Found

I found a _____
And what do you know?
My little _____ started to grow.

I found a _____
And what do you think?
My little _____ started to shrink.

I found a _____
And what do you say?
My little _____ ran away.

When I Sing

When I sing like a _____
My voice is so high.

When I sing like a _____
My arms want to fly.

When I sing like a _____
My voice is down low.

When I sing like a _____
I touch my big toe.

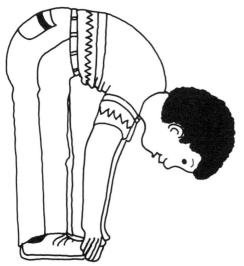

When I Dance

When I dance like a _____
I turn around.

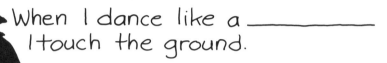

When I dance like a _____
I touch the ground.

When I twirl like a _____
My hands go up high.

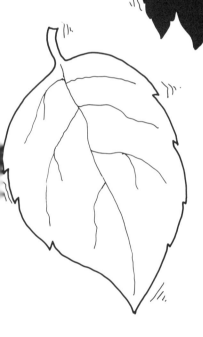

When I twirl like a _____
I reach to the sky.

When I leap like a _____
I wear a frown.

When I leap like a _____
I always fall down.

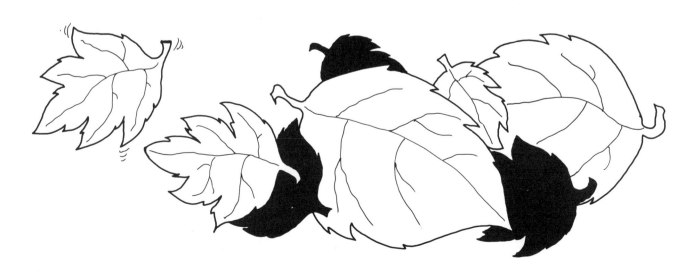

What Did I See?

I looked outside and what did I see?
A beautiful _____ smiling at me.

I looked up high and what did I see?
A colorful _____ smiling at me.

I looked in the box and what did I see?
A tiny, tiny _____ smiling at me.

Stop and Shop

The first stop's a _____ shop.
What will I buy today?
    A _____ for me
    A _____ for Mother
    A _____ for Sister and
    A _____ for Brother.
That's what I'll buy today.

The second stop's a _____ shop.
  What will I buy today?
    A _____ for me
    A _____ for Mother
    A _____ for Sister and
    A _____ for Brother.
That's what I'll buy today.

Continue with other types of shops.
Shop suggestions:
    fruit   hardware
    grocery   car
    shoe   flower
    toy   pet
    clothing   bakery

Birthday Cake

Baker, baker will you make
A great big _____ birthday cake.
_____ cake.
Make, make, make!
_____ cake.
Bake, bake, bake!
Here's your _____ birthday cake.

The children take turns naming their favorite birthday cake. Then the rest of the class pretends to be the baker, singing about making the cake.

Strange Animal

As I was walking down the street.
A strange little animal, I happened to meet.
He had a long _____.
And two big _____.
His fur was all _____.
   And he walked like a _____.
   He liked to eat _____.
   On the top of his head was a _____.
   He looked so silly, so different and new
   I knew right away, he belonged at
      the zoo!

The Parade

Here comes the parade
Marching down the street
Everyone is waving
At everyone they meet.

First comes the _____
Keeping in a line.

Next comes the _____
Looking really fine.

On top of the
   elephant
A little _____
   rides.

Then I see the
_____
Coming down both sides.

The _____ are
   exciting
I love them like the rest.

But if you really want to know
I love the _____ best.

Choosing a Pie

I went to the bakery
To buy a pie
Which one to choose?
Oh me, oh my!
The biggest was a _____ pie.
The sweetest was a _____ pie.
The tallest was a _____ pie.
The juiciest was a _____ pie.
The smallest was a _____ pie.
The one I bought was a _____ pie.
Home from the bakery
With my pie
Can't wait to finish dinner.
And you know why!

Giant Mess

As I went walking down the street.
A giant _____ I happened to meet.
He looked so lonely, so very sad
I took him home, which made him glad.
I hid him in _____ during the day.
Then let him out at night, to romp and play.
I couldn't keep my secret for long
For my giant _____ was ever so strong.
He pushed down the door and started to roam
Upstairs and down in our home.
He broke all the _____.
He stepped on the _____.
He sat on the _____.
He rolled over the _____.
He squashed the _____.
My mother came running, my dad came
    too.
And before you knew it, he was in
    the zoo!
So if you're out walking down the
    street.
And if a giant _____ you
    happen to meet.
Think twice before taking that
    _____ home.
'Cause you never know where he'll
    decide to roam!

SOLUTIONS

Baby Bird

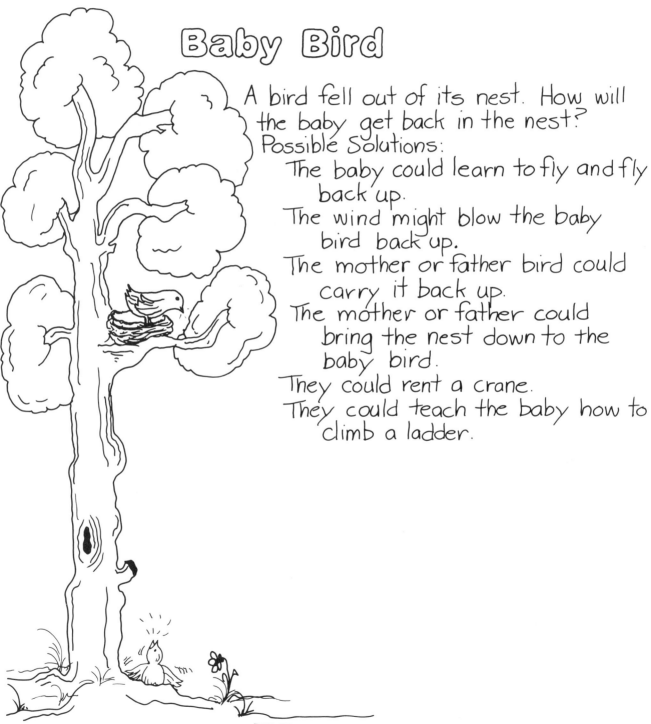

A bird fell out of its nest. How will the baby get back in the nest?

Possible Solutions:

The baby could learn to fly and fly back up.

The wind might blow the baby bird back up.

The mother or father bird could carry it back up.

The mother or father could bring the nest down to the baby bird.

They could rent a crane.

They could teach the baby how to climb a ladder.

The Picnic

The children have come to the park for a picnic. When they unpack their lunch, they find that they have forgotten the paper cups. How can they drink the juice that they have brought in their cooler?

Possible Solutions:

Go home and get the cups.

Make cups out of paper plates.

Wait to drink when they get home.

Cup their hands.

Stick straws into the cooler.

Go to the store and buy some cups.

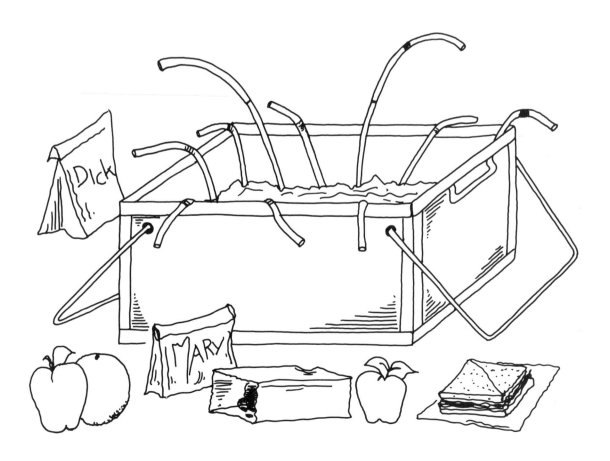

Here to There

Name a place that is nearby or in the same building where you are —the sandbox, let's say. Ask your children to think of different ways to get from where you are to the other place.

Possible Solutions:

Go down the hall and out the back door.

Go through the window and around the house.

Go out the front door, around the block, and then back through the yard.

You can also play this type of game with your children using a large map board. Have two or three children start at one point and all try to find different routes to the same destination.

Wonder Why

Take advantage of any unusual situations that you and your children observe. Say you see a family traveling in a car with a bird cage tied to the roof. Encourage your children to make up reasons **why**.

Possible Solutions:

They have lost their pet bird and they are trying to catch a new one.

They are letting the wind clean out the cage.

They are using it for a radio antenna.

Their car is crowded and they could not fit it inside.

It smelled too much to carry in the car.

They are going through the car wash and they want to wash the cage at the same time.

Giant Pumpkin

Tell your children a tale about two children who grew a beautiful big pumpkin. The trouble was the pumpkin grew too big. The children wanted to take it to the County Fair and enter it in a pumpkin contest, but they couldn't budge it. What could they do?

Possible Solutions:

Rent a crane.

Get parents to help lift.

Roll it to the fair.

Carve out the middle to make it lighter.

Take a picture of it.

Roll it onto a blanket and pull it to the fair.

My Friend's Birthday

It is your friend's birthday and you do
not have any money. What can you give her
as a present?
Possible Answers:
   I can give her a hug and a kiss.
   I can make a picture for her.
   I can give her a toy I don't
      want any more.
   I can pick some wild flowers
      for her.
   I can bake some cookies
      for her.
   I can sing her a song.

Adapt this activity to a
parent's or sibling's
birthday if it is appropriate.

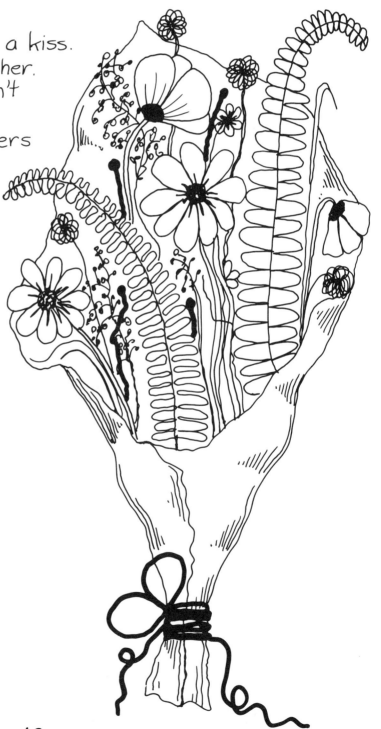

Ice Cream Store

Pretend that you are opening up a new ice cream store. Ask your children to help you invent some new flavors. Let the children take turns naming new flavors.

Examples:
pizza ice cream
cherry-banana ice cream
rainbow ice cream
Halloween ice cream (orange with chunks of licorice)
hot dog ice cream

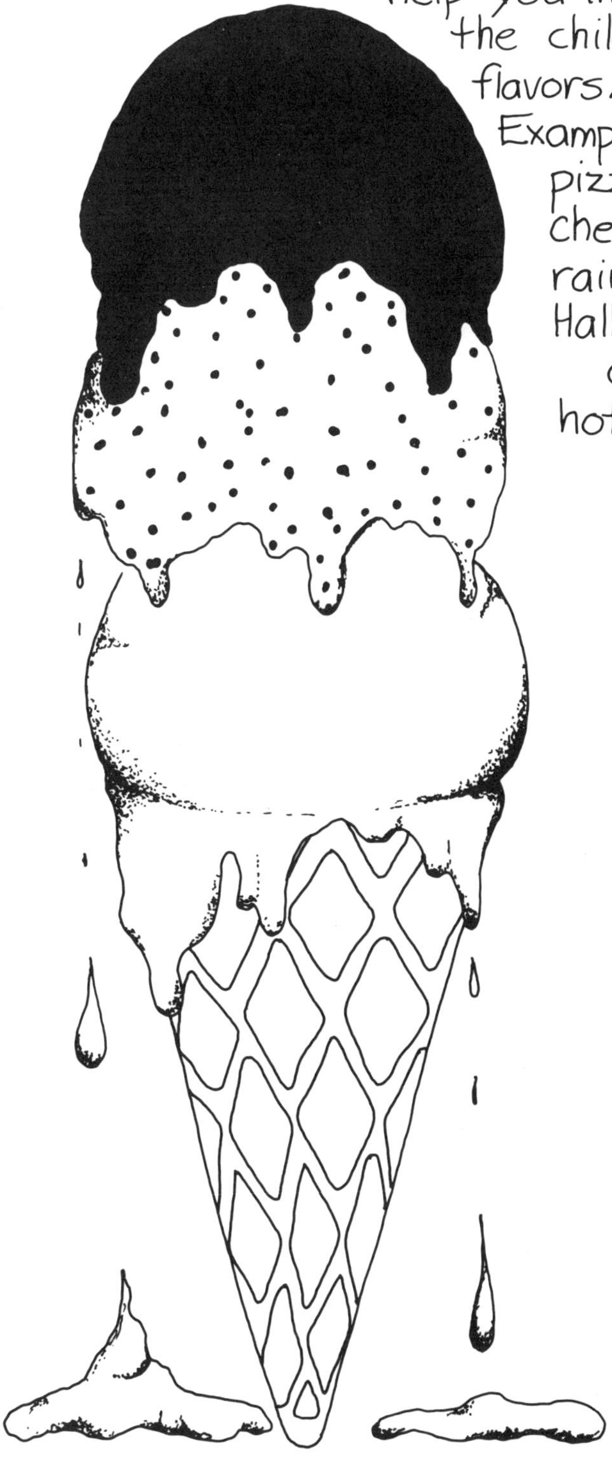

What's The Question?

Play a game with your children where you give them the "answer" and they have to think up a question that fits the answer. Example:

> You say **red**. Your child might answer "What color is my shirt?"

You may need to give the children many examples before they understand how the game is played. You can also begin by playing the game in reverse: Have your child give the 'answer' and you make up the question.

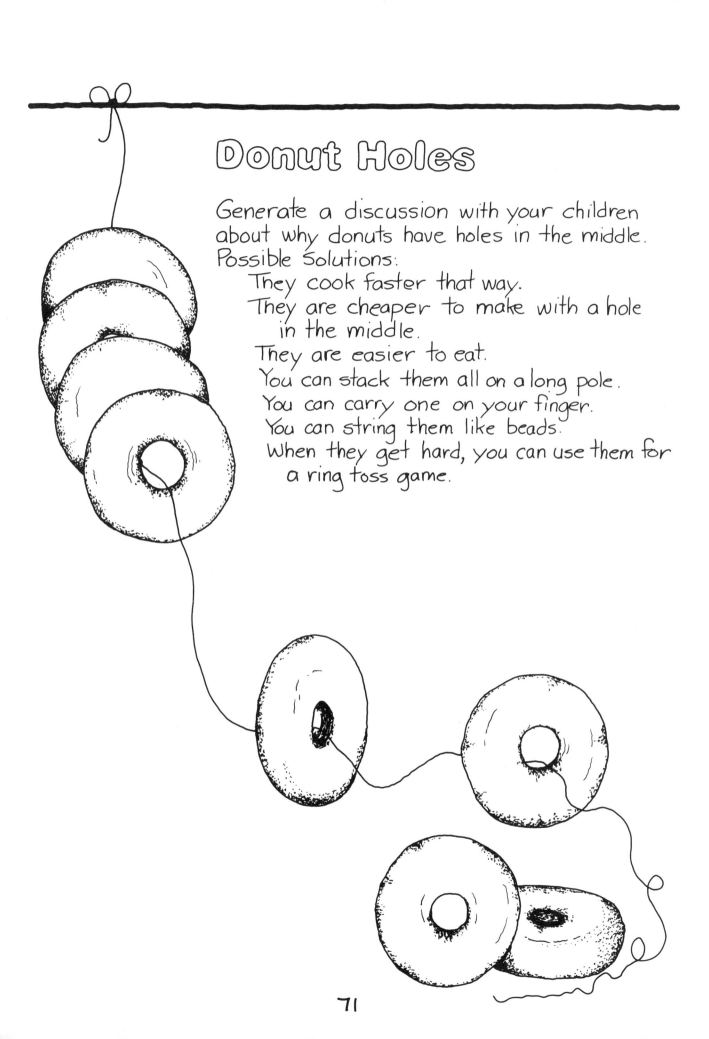

Donut Holes

Generate a discussion with your children about why donuts have holes in the middle.
Possible Solutions:

They cook faster that way.

They are cheaper to make with a hole in the middle.

They are easier to eat.

You can stack them all on a long pole.

You can carry one on your finger.

You can string them like beads.

When they get hard, you can use them for a ring toss game.

Christmas Tree Mystery

One day Mrs. Jones came home and found
her Christmas tree lying on the ground.
What could have happened?
Possible Solutions:

A cat jumped on the tree while chasing
a bird.
The baby pulled on an ornament.
Someone opened a window and the wind
blew it over.
A dog chased a cat up the tree.
A burglar knocked it over.
Santa Claus tripped over a toy and
fell on it.

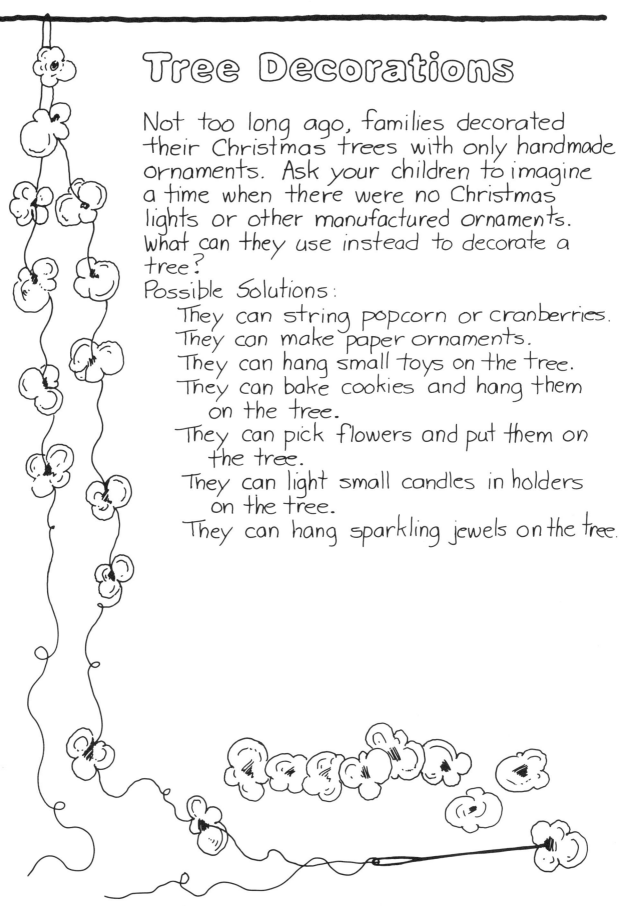

Tree Decorations

Not too long ago, families decorated their Christmas trees with only handmade ornaments. Ask your children to imagine a time when there were no Christmas lights or other manufactured ornaments. What can they use instead to decorate a tree?

Possible Solutions:

They can string popcorn or cranberries.
They can make paper ornaments.
They can hang small toys on the tree.
They can bake cookies and hang them on the tree.
They can pick flowers and put them on the tree.
They can light small candles in holders on the tree.
They can hang sparkling jewels on the tree.

Easter Bunny Problems

Oh-Oh! It's Easter time and the Easter Bunny has run out of egg dye. How else can he color his eggs?

Possible Solutions:

    Color them with crayons.
    Color them with marking pens.
    Wrap them with colored yarn.
    Dip them in beet juice.
    Paint them.
    Paste sequins on them.
    Cover them with glue and sprinkle
       on glitter.

The Easter Bunny has run out of eggs. What else can he put in his baskets?

Possible Solutions:

    He can put small toys in the basket.
    He can cut out paper eggs.
    He can bake cookies shaped like
       bunnies and eggs.
    He can put candy eggs in the
       baskets.
    He can put fruit in the
       baskets.
    He can put tennis balls
       in the baskets.

Easter Bunny Problems continued

The Easter Bunny has run out of artificial grass for his Easter baskets. What else can he use?

Possible Solutions:

He can shred newspapers.
He can cut up green tissue paper.
He can put in real grass.
He can use leaves.
He can put in cotton balls.
He can use Styrofoam packing "squiggles" or "peanuts."

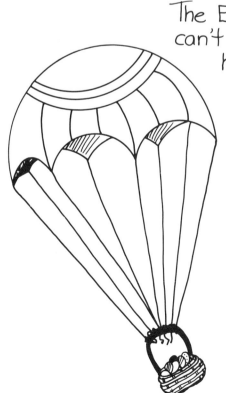

The Easter Bunny has broken his leg and can't hop very fast. How can he deliver all his baskets?

Possible Solutions:

He can hire an airplane and drop them from parachutes.
He can ride on a skateboard.
He can learn how to fly by flapping his ears.
He can send them in the mail.

How Many Ways?

How many ways can you get across the room?
How many ways can you say "Happy Birthday"?
How many ways can you keep cool in
    the summer time?
How many ways can you cook an egg?
How many ways can you go downstairs?
How many ways can you pop a balloon?
How many ways can you eat peanut butter?
How many ways can you show you are angry?
How many ways can you show you are happy?
How many ways can you get across a river?
How many ways can Santa get down a chimney?
How many ways can you catch a monster?
How many ways can you catch a fish?
How many ways can you play with a ball?
How many ways can you say "Thank you"?

Would You Rather?

Would you rather be an elephant or a mouse?
Would you rather be a mother or a father?
Would you rather be a bee or a flower?
Would you rather be a raindrop or a snowflake?
Would you rather be Little Red Riding Hood or
 Goldilocks?
Would you rather be a farm or fish?
Would you rather be hot or cold?
Would you rather work or play?
Would you rather watch a movie or a live play?
Would you rather eat spinach or liver?
Would you rather sing or dance?

Would you rather ride on a
 train or a plane?
Would you rather eat ice
 cream or cake?
Would you rather it was
 Christmas or Hanukah,
  or your birthday?
Would you rather
  live in an igloo or
  a tipi?

What If?

What if you had your own robot?
What if you broke your best friend's favorite toy?
What if your teddy bear could sing and dance?
What if it rained all the time?
What if everything around you was the same color?
What if you had no car? How would you get places?
What if animals could talk? What would your
    pet say?
What if everyone looked the same? What
    would the world be like?
What if you were no bigger
    than your thumb? What
    would your life be like?
What if you lived in a house
    made of ice? What would it
    be like?
What if money grew on trees?
    What would you do?
What if the world was
    totally covered with water?
    What would life be like?
What if people could not talk?
    How would they
    communicate?
What if you could fly? Where
    would you go?
What if it never got dark?
    What would the world be
    like?

Mother Goose What Ifs

Mary had a little lamb
Its fleece was white as snow
And everywhere that Mary went
The lamb was sure to go.

What might happen if Mary's lamb followed
her into a store?

Jack and Jill went up the hill
To fetch a pail of water.
Jack fell down and broke his crown
And Jill came tumbling after.

If Jack's pail broke, what else could he use
to fetch water with?

Mary, Mary, quite contrary
How does your garden grow?
With silver bells and cockel shells
And little maids all in a row.

What else could Mary grow in
her garden if she had space?

Relationships

How is a rainbow like a mountain?
Possible answers:
    They are both high.
    They are both curved.

How is a chair like a frog?
Possible answers:
    They both have legs.
    They are both squat.

How is a flower like a shoe?
Possible answers:
    They come in different colors.
    They both smell!

How is a house like a car?
Possible answers:
    They both have windows and doors.
    They both have heaters.

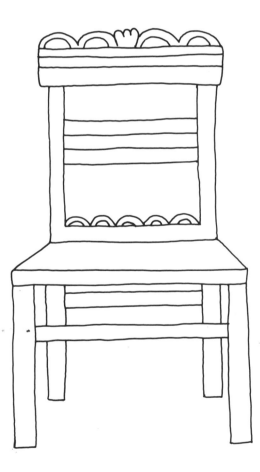